TOM P

READING THE GAME

Illustrated by
Brian Williamson

PUFFIN

PUFFIN BOOKS

Published by the Penguin Group
Penguin Books Ltd, 80 Strand, London WC2R 0RL, England
Penguin Group (USA) Inc., 375 Hudson Street, New York, New York 10014, USA
Penguin Group (Canada), 90 Eglinton Avenue East, Suite 700, Toronto, Ontario, Canada M4P 2Y3
(a division of Pearson Penguin Canada Inc.)
Penguin Ireland, 25 St Stephen's Green, Dublin 2, Ireland (a division of Penguin Books Ltd)
Penguin Group (Australia), 250 Camberwell Road, Camberwell, Victoria 3124, Australia
(a division of Pearson Australia Group Pty Ltd)
Penguin Books India Pvt Ltd, 11 Community Centre, Panchsheel Park, New Delhi – 110 017, India
Penguin Group (NZ), 67 Apollo Drive, Rosedale, North Shore 0632, New Zealand
(a division of Pearson New Zealand Ltd)
Penguin Books (South Africa) (Pty) Ltd, 24 Sturdee Avenue, Rosebank, Johannesburg 2196, South Africa

Penguin Books Ltd, Registered Offices: 80 Strand, London WC2R 0RL, England

puffinbooks.com

First published 2009
006

Text copyright © Tom Palmer, 2009
Illustrations copyright © Brian Williamson, 2009
All rights reserved

Set in 14.5/21pt Baskerville MT by Palimpsest Book Production Limited,
Grangemouth, Stirlingshire
Made and printed in England by Clays Ltd, St Ives plc

British Library Cataloguing in Publication Data
A CIP catalogue record for this book is available from the British Library

ISBN: 978-0-141-32470-8

www.greenpenguin.co.uk

For Nikki Woodman

Contents

Teamwork

Ben could see what Ryan was going to do before he did it. He knew how his friend liked to play football.

Ryan would trap the ball, then look up, ready to play it forward. To his left, or to his right.

He always did that.

So Ben sprinted up the pitch, his arm in the air, shouting, 'Ryan!' And, just as he thought, Ryan controlled the ball and played it forward to Ben's feet.

1

Now Ben had three options: run with the ball, pass it back to Ryan, or play in another team-mate who was moving forward too.

Ben knew who would be moving forward.

Yunis would be making a direct run into the area.

Will would be drifting to the far post.

And Jake would be in the space behind

the Manchester City defenders on the other
side of the pitch.

He looked up. The defenders had gone
with Yunis and Will, back-pedalling
desperately. As a result, Jake was in loads
of space.

So Ben played it to Jake, cutting the
Manchester City defence in half.

Ben could see what would happen next
too. United would score.

Jake took the ball to the touchline,
side-stepped his defender and slid the ball
to Yunis's feet.

Yunis did the rest, clipping the ball in.
Low and hard. The Manchester City defence
was all over the place.

One–one.

That was better. At least they weren't
losing now.

This was an important game, the first for

the under-twelves since coming back from a tournament in Poland a week ago.

United's under-twelves were all really good players. The best in their region. United were a top side in the Premiership and some of this under-twelves team were expected to become professionals in a few years' time. Maybe even internationals.

Ben watched Jake and Yunis celebrating in the penalty area. They always looked odd together. Little and large. Jake was small and thin; Yunis tall and muscular. The two of them turned and did a thumbs up to Ben.

Ben smiled. He loved playing with these two. He knew their games so well. They were good players: always in the right place at the right time.

Then Ben looked at the parents, a row of figures in cagoules and jumpers on the far side. They were standing behind a narrow

bar that ran along the length of the pitch,
on the opposite side to the United coaches
and substitutes.

Then Ben saw his own family.

His mum, standing behind the pushchair.
The baby, Tom, all wrapped up. His brother
and sister, Cameron and Molly, laughing
and waving.

Ben's mum waved to him and grinned. She knew he'd set the goal up. She *knew* about football. She'd taught him how to play when he was younger than Molly or Cameron, when he was her only child. After his first dad had walked out and left them.

Ben gave his attention back to the game. Now United could try to win it.

They'd been a goal down since the first minute, when James, the central defender, had made a terrible mistake, letting one of the Manchester City attackers break into the penalty area, unmarked.

It was so out of character for James to let something like that happen. But Ben knew that everyone made mistakes. Even the team's best player, which James definitely was, as well as being the son of a former England international.

Manchester City retrieved the ball for the kick-off. There were ten minutes left.

Ryan came over to Ben.

'Nice one, Ben,' he said. 'That ball you played to Jake. Not bad.'

'Cheers,' Ben said, beaming.

Ben was always happy to get praise from Ryan. He was the team captain. And a good mate. They were in the same class at school too.

Sometimes Ryan could be a bit mean to the other players. But recently – since United had been back from Poland – he'd been a lot better. Less likely to make trouble.

But Ben knew he had to focus on the game. It was still one all.

Manchester City were about to kick off. United could still win it. Or lose it.

Sunday 27 November
United 1 Manchester City 1
Goals: Yunis
Bookings: Craig, James

Under-twelves manager's marks out of ten for each player:

Tomasz	6
Connor	7
James	4
Ryan	6
Craig	5
Chi	6
Sam	7
Will	6
Jake	7
Yunis	7
Ben	7

Big Brother

After the final whistle, the parents were allowed to talk to the boys. Ben's mum came over immediately and hugged him.

Then Molly hugged him. And Cameron. Tom had fallen asleep, but Ben touched his face.

'Well played, Ben,' Mum said. 'You were really good today. Man of the match.'

'Thanks,' he said, trying to get out of being hugged.

He was shocked. His mum was always supportive, but she'd never said that before. Not in all his thirty or forty games for United over the last three years. If she'd said it, she meant it.

Mum looked at her watch. 'I'm sorry, though, love. I need to be off in five minutes.'

This was *not* new.

After home games Ben's mum sometimes had to go to work, at a cafe in the town centre. She brought the kids to watch the

game, then Ben had to take them home
and sort their food out. And entertain them.
All afternoon.

'Fine,' Ben said. 'I'll be changed in no
time.'

He ran to the dressing rooms, slung his kit
in his bag and got changed. No time for
a shower.

Then he was off.

As he was leaving, Steve Cooper – the
team manager – came in. He was a big man,
with wild dark hair and a deep booming
voice.

'Got to look after the kids?' Steve said.

'Yeah. Sorry.'

'No worries,' Steve said. 'No dads
around?'

'Neither of them.' Ben shrugged.

'Well, I'll catch up with you later,' Steve
said. 'But I just want to say you played really

well today, Ben. That goal was down to you. All that hard work you've been doing in training is really paying off, isn't it?'

Ben nodded, smiling.

'Go on,' Steve said. 'Go.'

Ben raced outside. Molly and Cameron flung themselves at him, just as his team-mates were trooping back from the pitches. Ben loved this, having two younger siblings who worshipped him in front of all his friends.

His mum handed him the house keys and turned the pushchair round for him.

'Thanks, love,' she said.

It was only a ten-minute walk to get the kids home. Ben would have to think of things to do with them until his mum came back at teatime.

He looked over at a group of his

team-mates standing near the building that made up United's training facilities. They had the afternoon off now. They were free to do what they wanted: watch the match on satellite TV, play on their computers or go round to their mates'. Sometimes he envied them.

'Shall we go home?' Ben said.

'Poo,' Molly said, grinning wickedly, as they walked past Yunis and Jake.

'What?' Ben said, catching Jake's eye. Jake was grinning too.

'Poo,' Molly said again.

'Poo,' Cameron said, louder.

'Molly. Cameron. Stop it.'

'Poo! Poo! Poo! Poo! Poo!'

'Stop it,' Ben whispered, kneeling down. They were alone now, on the way down to the main road. There was a line of trees, then a row of fences protecting several training pitches.

'Why?' Cameron said.

'You can't say that,' Ben said. 'Not in front of other people.'

'Wee,' Molly said.

'Molly!'

'*You* say "poo",' Cameron said. 'And "wee".'

Ben nodded. 'I do, but not in front of other people.'

'Why?'

'Why can't we say "poo"?' Cameron added.

'It's rude,' Ben said.

'But *you* say it,' Cameron said again.

'Only to you two,' Ben whispered. 'Not to anyone else.'

'Can we say it now?' Molly said.

Ben looked down the road, then behind them, and nodded. 'Yes, now it's just us you can. But quietly.'

'Poo,' Molly said.

'Wee wee,' Cameron said.

'Bog.'

'Plop plop.'

'Sick.'

Ben grinned. He had thought it was funny teaching his younger siblings some rude – but not *very* rude – words. Now he was starting to regret it.

Panic

'Right, lads.'
Steve Cooper had gathered the
squad together, sitting on the grass
in a goalmouth. It was Monday
evening.

The training pitches were next to a large
wood and alongside a river. On the other side
of the river there was a stately home with
posh gardens and a visitors' centre. Ben had
visited the place several times as a young boy.

They had warmed up with runs and

some close passing, and now Steve was addressing them.

'First of all: the game yesterday,' he said. 'Very good. Maybe we didn't win, but the teamwork was great. The way you played together: excellent. And I thought Ben had a great match. He really read the game superbly. I was very pleased.'

Ben grinned and looked at Ryan. This felt good. He liked being praised, especially in front of the rest of the team.

Ryan made a face like he was angry with Ben, but then he grinned.

'Here's what we're going to do tonight,' Steve said. 'More work on options in front of the goal. Trying to set yourself up so you can cope with more than one thing happening.'

Steve arranged the boys in groups in the penalty area, with Tomasz in goal.

Each boy had to run towards the penalty area, and Steve – standing on the penalty spot – would throw the ball to either his left or right. Then the player had to shoot first time.

The idea was to predict which way Steve would throw the ball, then to adjust your footing if you got it wrong. And, of course, to score.

In the dressing rooms after training, Craig and Chi were holding a sheet of paper.

Chi was a midfielder too, a calm player, one of the more experienced boys at United. Craig was a defender and the team joker.

'Ben, have you seen this?' Chi asked.

'It's a match report on yesterday,' Craig added. 'It's all about you. Ben Blake this . . . Ben Blake that . . .'

Ben smiled. This was great – more praise. He could get used to this. He wanted one of them to read it to him.

Then Craig came across and handed it to Ben.

Ben felt his heart begin to race, but he took the sheet of paper. This was what he knew he was meant to do. He sat down and stared at the sheet, which was covered in words. He nodded and smiled for a minute or so – taking as long as he thought it might take to read it. Then he made to hand it back to Craig.

But Craig looked surprised. 'What about the end bit?'

'What?' Ben said. He was feeling sick now. He looked at the page again. The words were swimming across it. In his panic, he couldn't make *any* of them out.

'The end bit. Read it.'

'I'll . . . I'll read it later,' Ben stammered.

'Later? Read it now. It's about *you*.'

Ben could feel his face and the skin around his neck getting hot. This was his worst nightmare come true. Everyone at school knew he was stupid. But at the Academy people thought he was OK. Even clever.

Now he was about to lose the one last place in the world where people didn't think he was stupid.

'Get lost, Craig. If I don't want to read it, I won't. OK?'

Ben moved forward and pushed past Craig.

Craig looked confused, staring at Ben in disbelief. And Ben could only stand there like a statue, not knowing what to do or say next.

And then the paper was snatched from his hand.

Ben turned, ready to fight now. If someone was going to mock him he'd get the first blow in.

But it was Ryan. The only one who could help.

'Let's have a look,' Ryan said, not stopping to let anyone else speak. 'Blah blah blah . . . "*Ben Blake had his best game yet for the under-twelves*" . . . blah blah blah . . . "*his reading of the game was as good as you'd expect from an under-eighteen*" . . . blah blah blah . . . "*United will have high hopes he'll make it as a professional if he carries on showing this level of maturity . . .'"*

Ben didn't know what to feel. Thrilled to have such things said about him? Stupid, for pushing past Craig? Or sick with shame that Ryan was standing there reading it out for him.

Because Ben had this thing. A secret that his busy mum and his absent dads – even his teachers – didn't know about.

Ben couldn't read.

After Ben had gone home, Steve, the team manager, took Ryan aside. Ryan was used to being taken aside by Steve, mainly because he was forever getting into trouble. But also because he was team captain and Steve looked to him to sort out minor problems.

Ryan assumed it was because he'd done something to annoy Steve. But he was wrong.

'What was all that about earlier?' Steve said.

'All what?' Ryan replied.

'With Ben.'

'Oh, that,' Ryan said. 'Just a scuffle. Nothing.'

'Why was Ben so upset?'

Ryan shrugged. There was no way he was going to give up Ben's secret. 'Nothing. Just stuff. You know,' he said.

'And he's all right at school?' Steve asked.

'Yeah,' Ryan said, knowing he didn't sound convincing. Ben was not all right at school, far from it. Ryan had to help him with his reading and writing, something nobody else knew.

'OK then . . .' Steve raised an eyebrow and headed back inside.

Class War

*I*f Ben was at his happiest playing and training for United, he was at his unhappiest at school. And things had got worse since he'd come to high school. Much worse. Primary school had been bearable, but there was no hiding from his reading problems now he was in year seven.

There were thirty eleven- and twelve-year-olds in English the morning after training. Ben always sat next to Ryan, but this week they'd been split up for messing about.

And that meant problems. Big problems.

Ben didn't know how he was going to get through the lesson without his friend. And to make it worse, they had a supply teacher this morning, Mrs Pritchard, a teacher who Ben couldn't work out. She was either nervous or she hated children – he couldn't decide.

'OK,' Mrs Pritchard said. 'Let's settle down.'

No one settled down.

'Year seven?'

Barely anyone was listening. Half the class were still talking. But Ben wasn't. He was sitting at his table, eyes fixed on the teacher, trying to be good. Trying not to stand out.

Ryan was standing on his chair, shouting. Several people watched him, grinning.

'What's your name?' the supply teacher shouted.

Ryan turned and smiled. 'Ryan,' he said.

'Ryan. Detention. This lunchtime.'

Ryan scowled at the teacher, then turned to sit down. And – with that – the rest of the class went quiet.

'OK, class. Thank you.'

Ben frowned. Mrs Pritchard had a way

of saying thank you as if it was the last thing she meant.

'Now,' Mrs Pritchard went on, 'let's take up from the book you were reading with Mrs Nash. She left me a note somewhere.' The teacher shuffled through a stack of papers. 'Ah, yes. Here we are. Page one hundred and thirty-seven.'

Twenty-nine children groaned; Ben sat in stony silence.

*

Thirty minutes later, they were still reading. They had to read a page each, round the class. They were on page 163.

Ben had actually been enjoying the novel, so long as other people were reading it to him. He liked stories. He even tried to follow the text with his finger. But the words looked like a jumble of letters to him most of the time.

With five minutes of the lesson left, there were only two people to read before Ben. Ben had had high hopes they'd get to lunch before it was his turn to read, but he was becoming less and less sure that was going to happen.

He started to think of ways he could get out of it.

Then Julie Tipper finished reading.

'Thank you,' Mrs Pritchard said. 'Now,

let's hear from you.' She pointed at Brian Kendrew.

There was a silence, then a slow, croaking voice. 'I'm not feeling well, Miss. Can I not read, please?'

Brian's voice sounded bad, like he had a sore throat.

Ben felt panic. His legs went weak. He could feel sweat on his forehead.

'Fine,' Mrs Pritchard said. 'Who's next?' The supply teacher pointed at Ben.

'I'm not . . . well, either,' Ben said, stumbling over his words.

'You sound fine to me.'

'I feel ill,' Ben insisted.

'Can I read instead?' A voice came across the room. Ryan's voice.

'Thank you, Ryan . . .' the teacher said, and Ben felt a rush of relief: he owed his friend. Big time.

'But you've contributed enough already, Ryan.' Mrs Pritchard turned to look at Ben. 'And I'd very much like to hear *you* read.'

'I'm not reading,' Ben said. 'I don't want to.'

Ben looked across the aisle at Brian Kendrew, who was grinning at the boy next to him. Then Brian made a face, a face that said '*Ben Blake's dumb, stupid, a thicko*'.

Ben knew that face. He'd seen it too many times before.

'Ben, I've asked you to read,' Mrs Pritchard said. 'All the other children have read. Why should you be any different from them?' The teacher's voice was calm.

Ben looked at Ryan, who was staring back at him, helpless. Ryan always got him out of these situations. Sometimes he read, pretending to be Ben, fooling teachers. Sometimes he caused trouble to distract the teachers.

But not today. He was already on a detention and he couldn't push it any further.

Ben heard whispers behind him. Mutterings. He thought he heard someone else say '*Thicko*'. He turned to see Brian Kendrew grinning at him again.

And – with that – something snapped in his head.

Ben lunged across the aisle at Brian Kendrew, papers scattering across the classroom, a girl screaming.

Steve at School

Ryan was outside the PE block – pushing a lad from 7C about – when he saw Steve walking up the drive from the school gates, towards reception. He suspected that Steve had seen him doing it. It'd only been a laugh, not a fight or anything like that. But he didn't want Steve to think he'd been bullying anyone. That could lead to all sorts of trouble.

And, anyway, what was Steve doing here?

Ryan wanted to find out. He went along the front of the school, past rows of windows, some with blinds down so you couldn't see inside. He looked into the offices. And that was when he saw Steve talking to his head of year, Mrs Nash.

What was going on?

Ryan panicked. It must be to do with Poland. And him.

A couple of weeks ago, on the club trip to Warsaw, Ryan had got into some trouble for being mean to Tomasz. Was Steve talking to his teachers about it? And if he was, what was he going to do?

Ryan knew he'd been stupid. He'd said he was sorry. He'd tried to make it up to Steve and Tomasz, say he'd not be like that again. And he really meant it. But it looked like he hadn't done enough.

He wished Ben was here. But Ben had been off – probably playing truant – since yesterday morning. He'd hit Brian Kendrew, right in front of the supply teacher.

Ryan waited and watched. He was nervous. This could affect him at United – seriously.

*

Two hours later, Ryan left school under a cloud, walking down the school drive, through the trees, to the shops at the bottom of the hill.

He was worried. Really worried. What would happen when he got to training that

night? Would Steve be waiting for him? He thought he'd done enough to show Steve that he would stop being a bully. But maybe Steve was still going to do something. Like what? Throw him out of the club? Take the captaincy from him? Again. Why else would he be going to school?

While he was thinking, Ryan heard running footsteps behind him. He turned. It was Ben.

'How was it?' Ben said.

'What? School?'

'Yeah.'

'OK.' Ryan wondered if he should tell Ben about seeing Steve. He was still feeling funny about it.

'I need a favour,' Ben said, interrupting his thoughts.

'What?'

'Can you help me do the shopping?' Ben

said. 'Before training. You can have tea at ours.'

'Sure,' Ryan said. 'Have you got the list off your mum?'

'Yeah.'

They'd done this before. Ben had to get some food from the shops. He knew what most things were without reading them, but there were new things on the list today – words he didn't recognize.

They went into a small supermarket. There were three aisles of food and cleaning products in boxes, bottles and tubes.

As they were shopping, Ryan decided to tell Ben about Steve.

'What?' Ben said. 'At school? I thought he trained the first team in the day.'

'Me too,' Ryan said.

'Did he see you?'

'I don't think so,' Ryan said.

'Maybe he's just checking up. On both of us,' Ben said. 'United have to keep in touch with our school. It's part of the deal.'

'Yeah, but I've never seen him at school before,' Ryan said. 'And no one else has ever had him come to their school. Have they ever said so to you?'

'No,' Ben said. And he wondered what was going on.

Anticipation

'Right, lads,' Steve said, standing with his hands on his hips, staring at the fourteen young footballers in front of him. 'Today we're going to work on anticipation.'

Steve looked at each of the lads in turn. Nobody spoke.

'Who can tell me what anticipation means?'

Ben's hand shot up.

'Ben?'

'Knowing what is going to happen – but before it does happen.'

'Yes. Exactly,' Steve said. 'And you, Ben, are one of the best at it.'

Steve rubbed his hands together. It was cold tonight. The coldest training day of the season so far, and the floodlights were on. It was the last day of November.

Steve explained the drill. They were going to play seven-a-side. A normal game, but with a difference.

If Steve blew the whistle, everybody had to stop dead. Then Steve would ask the player with the ball some questions. Where were his team-mates? What were his best options? Who could he play it to on their team to advance the game? And whoever it was had to do this without looking.

The training game kicked off. They played as normal until a shrill whistle went.

'Right. Chi, shut your eyes. Where is . . . James?'

Chi paused. 'Behind me?' he said, unsure.

The rest of the lads started laughing.

Chi opened his eyes. James was three paces in front of him.

'Good try, Chi,' Steve said. 'This drill is about knowing where your team-mates are. It's a hard thing to get used to. But we need to know where everyone is so that you can anticipate what to do next. The game is about more than where *you* are: it's about where your team-mates are. And knowing that.'

They started again. Steve blew his whistle two minutes later. 'Ben, shut your eyes.'

Ben stood still, his eyes shut.

'Where is Connor, Ben?'

'On the edge of the penalty area, in the space behind Yunis,' Ben said.

'Excellent,' Steve said.

Ben opened his eyes. He'd been right. Spot on.

After training, Steve came over to Ben as he was leaving the pitch.

'How's it going, Ben? I thought you were excellent tonight. You worked really hard and showed great vision.'

'Cheers,' Ben said. 'I'm loving it.'

'What about everything else? How's your mum? School?'

Ben stopped walking for a second, making Steve turn and stop too. It was

weird: whenever he was at the Academy, Ben would forget everything – all his worries – as if school didn't exist. Until someone had to mention it.

'Fine,' Ben said, walking again.

'You know, we're here to help you,' Steve said. 'We're not just football coaches. We can support you with other stuff too.'

Ben wondered what he meant. He thought about asking if Steve would do a bit of babysitting for his mum, for a joke, but decided not to.

'What I mean to say, Ben, is that we're here. Be it something to do with football, something to do with your home life, something to do with school.'

Ben nodded quickly. 'Cheers,' he said again.

'Don't forget,' Steve said.

Ben nodded again, then headed off with

the rest of the team into the dressing rooms, wondering what that was all about.

What with this and Ryan seeing Steve at school, Ben could sense something was going on.

The Shot

A nother Sunday afternoon, another game. But this game was weird.

Weird because it was going exactly the same way the last game had gone: a bad mistake by James early on, followed by a piece of amazing skill by Ben.

It was United 1 Everton 1.

James's mistake had been a shock. Tomasz had bowled the ball out to him from the goal and James had turned with it, to play it forward to Craig. But he'd mis-cued it. The ball had trickled across the eighteen-yard box for an Everton forward, who only needed one touch before he knocked it past Tomasz.

One–nil.

Easy. Too easy.

But then – just before half-time – Ben was tracking Will, who was marked by two Everton players and had nowhere to go.

Will looked like he was about to play it back to the United defence until Ben made his run, anticipating Will's problem.

Ben ran towards the ball, drawing one of the Everton defenders away from Will. Then Ben changed direction and ran towards the goal again.

Will saw his move and chipped the ball over him.

Suddenly Ben was in miles of space. He controlled the ball, turned and moved towards goal, eyes up.

That was when he saw Yunis moving, as he expected, into the penalty area. Jake was sprinting behind Yunis, on the left wing. Two of the Everton defenders had gone with Yunis, and that left Jake free.

Ben clipped the ball over Yunis – and the defenders – to Jake. The defenders stopped, one running towards him. Jake trapped the ball and slid it into Yunis, who was now unmarked.

Yunis did the rest.

One–one.

The second half was tight. No one wanted to make mistakes. There was a nervousness in both United's and Everton's play.

Ben knew what was happening. He'd seen it before. An atmosphere had come over the game, one that meant each player didn't want to be seen to make a mistake. It was like you sometimes got in major cup finals – that was why so many of them ended in penalties.

Ben thought back to Poland. If they'd been playing in that kind of atmosphere – where each game was competitive – someone would have tried to win the game. But this was a friendly. They never played competitive matches, unless it was a special tournament.

It was part of what professional clubs did with juniors: it wasn't about winning – it was about developing the players to be as good as they could be.

So Ben decided to take a risk. He wanted the game to liven up.

The next time he got the ball, he decided that, wherever he was, he would shoot. The keeper had been off his line for most of the half, nearer the penalty spot than the goal.

Two minutes later he called for the ball and Ryan knocked it to him.

Ben turned and – without pausing to think – hit the ball as hard as he could, high, over the keeper.

At home he had a DVD of the greatest Premiership goals. There was one by David Beckham. Against Wimbledon, wasn't it? He'd been in his own team's half, but had just lobbed the ball into the net. Amazing.

Ben's shot lofted over the Everton midfield and defence, then came plunging out of the sky like the Beckham shot.

Everyone had stopped running to watch. Both teams. The referee. Even the Everton keeper.

But Ben began to run. Towards the goal.

Questions had started coming into his

head. What if the ball didn't go in? What if it hit the bar – and came back into play?

Anticipation.

So as everyone stood and gazed at his shot, Ben ran.

Just in case.

The ball didn't hit the bar: it hit the left post. Then it hit the Everton keeper on the back of the head, bouncing out towards the

penalty spot. The keeper turned round, confused, not knowing where the ball was.

And there was Ben, on his own – no defenders for fifteen metres, the keeper looking the wrong way.

And he slotted it home.

Two–one.

Game over. And for once, with his aunt looking after his brothers and sister, Ben could spend some time with his team-mates after the game.

Sunday 4 December
United 2 Everton 1
Goals: Yunis, Ben
Bookings: Craig, Chi

Under-twelves manager's marks out of ten for each player:

Tomasz	6
Connor	6
James	5
Ryan	7
Craig	6
Chi	5
Sam	7
Will	6
Jake	6
Yunis	7
Ben	9

The Letter

Ben walked to the dressing rooms with Craig. Craig was a big lad, tall and wide, with wild hair. And Ben liked him – most of the time. The problem with Craig was that he was always trying to wind people up, but he was OK. Quite funny, really.

Today he was chipping away at Ben, as usual.

'You were rubbish today, Benny boy. Poor stuff. I reckon they'll have to let you go.'

Ben grinned. He'd just played his best game for United. He could handle this sort of teasing all day, because it just wasn't true. And they both knew it.

'That goal?' Ben said. 'Rubbish, was it? Could you do any better?'

'It was rubbish, Ben. Rubbish that it took you two shots,' Craig said. 'Any decent player

62

– me included – would have got the first one on target.'

Ben laughed. Craig was funny, so long as you were feeling confident.

And today he was. He was already fantasizing about what Steve and the others would say to him.

They walked over the bridge from the training pitches together. Their studs rattled on the wood and then the concrete of the car park.

As they came into the dressing room, Ben was expecting some serious praise. He'd just won United the game, single-handed – there was no doubting that.

But when he came in, the rest of the team were clustered in a circle round Chi. Ben wondered what they were going to do. Maybe shower him with Coke – pretending it was champagne? Something like that.

But he was wrong.

Chi shouted over to him. 'Look at this, Ben. This letter.'

Ben stopped walking, even took a step back. He felt that sick feeling again. This was dangerous. Why was this happening again, twice in a week? It was like someone was trying to show up the fact he couldn't read.

'What is it?' Ben said, as calmly as he could. He had to pretend nothing was wrong – that was his first rule. Only react when he had to.

'The letter. About the week before Christmas. Down south.' Chi was talking about the tournament United were to play against Arsenal, Chelsea and West Ham during the fixture break over Christmas.

'What does it say?' Ben asked.

'Have a look,' Chi said, putting the letter in Ben's hand.

Ben panicked. What now? He had to say something. He could feel his head going dizzy.

'I can't read that,' he said. 'I've just won the game for us. I don't want to read. *You* read it.' He dropped the paper on the floor, still panicking.

The room went quiet. And Ben knew

immediately that he sounded big-headed. No one ever boasted like that – it was a team game. But it was all he could think to say. He didn't mean it.

'Listen to Mr Superstar,' Craig said.

No one else spoke.

'I didn't mean that,' Ben said. 'It came out wrong.' He could feel the blood rushing to his face and his eyes were hot with embarrassment.

'Too important to read,' Craig said.

Ben felt like punching Craig. Why did he always do this? He picked on people at the wrong time, when they were at their most vulnerable.

Ben didn't know what to do. He picked up the piece of paper Chi had thrust at him. It was wet. He stared at it.

'I *will* read it,' he said. He could feel tears coming now, a swelling in his throat. He looked at the paper. He recognized some words, words he knew off by heart and didn't have to spell out letter by letter.

'West Ham,' he said. 'Chelsea. Arsenal.'

Chi said, 'Look at what it says about where we're staying.' He was being friendly, trying to help Ben. Chi was OK, a nice person.

But, however nice Chi was, Ben was still helpless. He couldn't read the rest of the sheet. No way.

'Come on, Benny boy,' Craig said, nudging Ben.

Ben barely heard him. All he could think was that being at United was his only retreat from not being able to read. United was where he could be himself and not worry about being singled out. But now that was over. He'd lost everything. Everybody would know he couldn't read.

Craig nudged Ben again and Ben looked at him. There was something in Craig's eyes, something that was mocking him.

'What?' Ben said.

'Read it.'

'No.' Ben was trying to keep a grip.

'Can't you?'

'What?'

'Can't you read?' Craig grinned. 'Are you a dumbo?'

Ben snapped. He shoved Craig hard on both shoulders and Craig fell down.

Then Ben walked out of the dressing room in his kit and boots, his school clothes in his bag. By the time he was outside, in the car park, he was struggling to hold back the sobs.

Losing Everything

'*B*en?'
　　Ben carried on walking, even though he could hear somebody calling his name. He walked across the car park and down the long lane that took you to the main road, past trees and grass and statues.

All Ben could see was the tarmac under his feet as he paced quickly away from his latest nightmare.

'BEN?'

It was Steve's voice.

Ben was going to carry on walking. He didn't want to stop for anyone. But then he heard running – quick heavy footsteps. Steve would catch up with him in seconds, so Ben stopped.

Steve put his hand on Ben's shoulder and Ben turned round. Then they were eye to eye.

'Are you OK?' Steve said.

'Yeah.'

'Why haven't you got changed?'

Steve was staring at Ben, who was still in his United kit. Ben noticed Steve's eyes flick to the crumpled-up letter in his hand. He'd forgotten he was still holding on to it.

'I need to get back,' Ben said. 'I'm looking after the kids.' He didn't even flinch at this lie. He was used to lying to cover up his problems.

'Right,' Steve went on. 'Well, I won't hold you up. I just wanted to talk to you. About home, school, all that. I think it could be useful.'

Ben shook his head. So Steve hadn't come after him because he'd pushed Craig? It was clear he didn't know. He was just being interested.

'No need,' Ben said in a quiet voice.

'I think there is, Ben. I was at your school on Wednesday. I saw Ryan. Didn't he tell you?'

'No,' Ben said. All he could think of was how difficult things had become. School and United were getting mixed up.

'I was talking to your head of year. She told me about your attendance record.'

That was it. It was over now. Ben could see his whole life falling apart. He had nothing left.

'I have to go,' Ben said to Steve. He was past caring what the team manager thought of him now. He wasn't even bothered if he offended Steve.

Steve said nothing for a moment. Then, 'Are you going to school tomorrow?'

Ben shrugged. 'Yeah,' he lied.

Steve nodded. Then he said, 'I can help.'

'I need to go,' Ben said again.

'OK.' Steve stepped back. 'I'll see you at training after school then.'

Ben shrugged again.

As Ben walked away from the training ground he wondered who he could talk to.

His mum? No way: she had enough to worry about with the kids and working in the cafe.

Ryan? Maybe. But he didn't want to load too much stuff on the one person who knew about him. Really knew about him.

His dad? That was the problem. He'd not

seen him for ages. If he had a proper dad –
like all his team-mates – he'd be OK. His dad
would help him, come to the matches, listen
to his problems. Teach him to read properly.

And Ben thought of his younger brothers
and sister. Who would teach them to read?
No one. Not if his mum was so busy and their
dad had gone, just like his had.

Ben imagined what it would be like to go
home now and read to the kids. He would
help them with the odd word, tell them
amazing stories. It would be brilliant. He
could do so much for them. Then they
wouldn't be like him, they wouldn't have to
feel like he felt in shops and in school and
today at United. Then they could be
different.

Cigarette?

Tuesday morning.
Ben left home at the time
he always did – as if he was
going to school. His mum shouted down
the stairs to him, 'Have a nice day at
school, love.'

Ben frowned. He still wasn't sure where
he was going to spend the day, or what he
was going to do. It had been a hard start to
the week. Missing school. And missing
training. He couldn't face either.

But he had a ball. And that was always a start.

A couple of streets from his house there was a small park. It had a bandstand, a few flower beds, a kids' playground. But it wasn't one his mum took the kids to.

There was also a wall. This wall had bricks that stuck out at an angle, which

meant that if you fired the ball against it, it could go left or right, or even come straight back at you. It was good practice for real football, good for testing your reflexes and your control.

When he got to the park, Ben began to hammer the ball against the wall. Each time it came back, he moved into the correct position, then trapped it.

He'd been doing it for over an hour when they came.

A group of lads, four of them. They were older than Ben, all smoking, and one was carrying a plastic bag that looked like it was full of cans of drink.

'Give us a kick,' the tallest lad said. He had thick black hair and was wearing blue tracksuit bottoms with expensive white trainers.

Ben passed him the ball. He decided it

would be best not to refuse – it would only lead to trouble.

But he felt scared, really scared. He knew he couldn't show it. He had to act like he was happy to be playing football with these lads, to show no fear.

The taller lad hoofed the ball, holding his cigarette behind him. The ball came back to Ben, so Ben passed it back to him.

The lad's three friends just watched.

After a couple of minutes of kicking the ball, the taller lad bent over and coughed. He seemed to be having trouble breathing.

Smoking, Ben thought. That's what happened if you smoked. Why did people do it? You'd be rubbish at football, for a start.

As the lad continued to cough, one of the other lads came over and offered Ben a cigarette.

'No thanks,' Ben said. There was no way

he was going to smoke. He wanted to be
able to breathe properly, and not to die in
agony.

But the cigarette lad's face looked angry,
like he really did want Ben to take a cigarette.

Ben was nervous now. What was he
supposed to do? Smoke – and go against
everything he thought was good for him?

Or maybe get into a fight with these four lads,
alone in this park?

Then he heard another voice, someone
calling his name.

'Ben?'

Ben turned to see a figure on a bicycle
speeding towards them.

'BEN!'

It was Steve.

Ben felt a rush of relief. Everything would
be OK now. Steve was here.

'What's going on?' Steve said, calling
Ben over.

The four older boys stood and watched,
blowing smoke into the air.

'I was just having a kick about,' Ben said.

'Are these your mates?'

'No. They just came.'

Steve looked at Ben's hands.

Ben shook his head vigorously. 'I'm not

smoking. They just came. I've been practising.' Ben pointed at the ball that was lying by the wall.

'You're going to have to deal with this school thing, Ben,' Steve said calmly. He picked up the ball and walked Ben away from the older boys.

Ben shrugged.

'It's going to affect you. At United. At home. Do you want to end up like that lot?' Steve asked. 'Or worse? You missed training yesterday. Was it to do with this?'

Ben looked at the ground. He could hear the four lads calling after him, but he couldn't make out their words. Steve's words meant more to him. Much more.

'How about a drink?' Steve said.

'What?'

'A drink.' Steve looked back at the older

boys. 'Not lager. Tea. How about a nice cup of tea?'

As they walked away, Ben heard the lads asking each other if Steve was that guy who used to play for United, the famous one. And Ben wondered why he was getting this special attention from Steve.

Maybe he was about to find out.

A Cup of Tea

Ben sat with his back to the window in the cafe and watched Steve at the counter. Two cups of tea.

Ben didn't like tea, but Steve had asked him what he wanted to drink from the menu and he'd panicked and said tea because that's what Steve had suggested in the park.

Steve sat down and looked at Ben. 'There's your drink,' he said.

'Thanks,' Ben said.

After a long pause, Steve said, 'Can I tell you a story?'

Ben nodded. What was this?

'You know I used to play for United?' Steve asked.

'Yeah.'

'Well, when I got there, just out of school in Bradford, I had a problem,' Steve said. 'I had to fill in some forms and sign my contract.'

'Right,' Ben said.

'Except I couldn't,' Steve said.

Ben nodded. He knew what this was about now. Somehow Steve knew about him and his reading.

'So the manager – you know, *the* manager?'

Ben knew who he meant: the legendary Scottish manager who'd won United the European Cup in the 1970s.

'Well, he took me aside and asked me straight, "Can you not read and write, son?" And I was petrified. I'd never told anyone. But I knew one thing: if I lied to the boss, it'd be a bad move. So I told him: I couldn't read *or* write.'

86

Ben leaned forward. He wanted to know what happened next. How had Steve made it to be so famous and clever – even though he couldn't read or write?

'You have to understand how I felt.' Steve paused. 'Well, I think you do. Nobody knew I was illiterate. That's what they called it. I had hidden it from my school, my family, everyone. And here I was admitting it. It was the hardest thing. But I knew – deep down, *I knew* – that this was the big moment for me. My whole future depended on this conversation.'

Ben nodded. He desperately wanted to know the end of this story.

'So, after training each day, the boss took me to his office –' Steve paused – 'and introduced me to his wife.'

Ben frowned. He'd not expected that. This was getting even more puzzling.

'And *she* taught me to read.' Steve took out a notebook and a pen. 'Can *you* read, Ben?'

Ben felt a chill run through him. He could feel his shoulders trembling. Steve was waiting, saying nothing. Why had he got a pen and pad out?

Ben wanted to say no: that he *couldn't* read or write. But it was like his mind was stuck in

mud. He looked down at his tea. He'd not
touched it. How many times had he had a
drink or some food in front of him in a cafe
that he didn't want? How many times had he
not done something because it might reveal
that he couldn't read?

Ben wanted to cry. But – like Steve had
known when he had his chance – Ben knew
this was his. He looked at Steve. If he'd
spoken, he'd have burst into tears, so he just
shook his head.

Steve wrote a word down on his pad.

Chelsea

'What does this say?' Steve said.
'Chelsea,' Ben said.
'What about this?'

Arsenal

'Arsenal,' Ben said.

'That's good,' Steve said. 'What about this?'

London

Ben stared at the word. He tried to work it out in his head, but he couldn't. He might as well have been looking at a group of symbols like:

*%&!%ᒥ

It meant nothing to him.

'I don't know,' Ben said, looking back into the cafe, feeling frozen inside.

'That's OK, Ben,' Steve said. 'You recognize words you have seen again and again, like football teams. You remember the

shape of the whole word, rather than the
sounds the letters make. But I can help you.
Like the boss's wife helped me.'

Steve wrote out some words on ten
separate pieces of paper from his notebook.

'Practise looking at these,' Steve said. 'See how you get on. We can go through them together tomorrow after training, if you want.'

Record Score

It was not easy going to the next match that Sunday.

Ben had been worrying all night. How would he avoid seeing Steve on his own? How would the others react to him after he'd hit Craig? And how would Craig react?

It was a problem.

So when he got up, he phoned Craig. He wanted to deal with this and get the problem out of the way.

'I'm sorry,' Ben said.

'It's all right,' Craig said. 'So am I.'

And that was it. That was Craig – straightforward. Sorted. Craig had sounded more interested in hearing that Ben was OK since he'd missed both training sessions in the week.

So Ben headed off to Ryan's, whose mum was giving them both a lift to Bradford for the match.

When Ben and Ryan got to the game – at Bradford's training camp – the rest of the team was quiet with Ben. So the first thing Ben did was go over to Craig and apologize in person. Craig gave Ben a pretend push and grinned. The other lads saw this – Craig had made sure.

Ben also made a point to talk to Chi, to make sure everything was OK, and it was.

Steve asked nothing about how Ben had got on with his words. So – as a result – the game went well.

James had called in sick, so Steve put an under-elevens defender, Matt, at the back. He was a big lad for his age and he was doing really well alongside Ryan. With less nerves in the defence, the midfielders, including Ben, had more time on the ball. Ben and Chi were working well down the right and Jake was tying the Bradford players in knots on the left.

Eleven minutes in, Ben got the ball out wide, after it had bounced off the back of a Bradford defender. He trapped it, paused and looked up. There was Yunis, attacking the goal. And Will too. But both were marked, so Ben played a high cross in to Craig, who was making a run from deep.

Craig leaped and headed it in.

One–nil.

Ben felt good that he'd set Craig up with a goal. He felt slightly less guilty for shoving him now.

The goals came easily after that. Bradford were poor, really poor. Holes appeared in their defence and Ben on one wing, Jake on the other, were finding lots of space to attack.

At half-time it was Bradford 0 United 4, and all the lads could talk about during the break was beating their record score: six–one.

'Come on. We can do it. Get seven. And

keep it tight at the back.' That was Ryan. He was going round to each player, firing them up.

Ben was happy for him. When they'd got back to England from the trip to Poland, Steve had said he'd drop him as captain, but the players had got together and asked Steve to give Ryan another chance. And Steve had agreed.

Ryan had turned into a model captain

overnight, not giving Tomasz any more trouble, not giving anyone trouble.

In the second half Will and Yunis scored again. Both were on two goals.

It was six–nil. One more goal and they'd have their record.

Ben saw the seventh goal coming before United even had possession.

A Bradford defender was about to play the ball forward to a midfielder but he'd under-hit it. Ben watched Chi run out of position to collect it. Ben went on to the shoulder of the last defender, trying to time his run so that he wouldn't be offside.

Then Ben saw Chi look up to spot him. Ben held his hand up and moved past the defender, just as Chi released the ball. A diagonal pass through the Bradford defence. Ben ran into the Bradford penalty area and the ball fell to his feet.

The linesman's flag stayed down and Ben volleyed the ball past the keeper.

Bradford 0 United 7. The team's record score.

And Ben had scored the seventh.

It was another great day for United and for their manager, Steve, who was applauding

on the touchline. He looked happy and proud.

Now all Ben had to do was get off the pitch and find his way home without bumping into Steve. He didn't want to talk about reading. He just wanted to go home.

Sunday 11 December
Bradford 0 United 7
Goals: Will 2, Yunis 2, Jake, Craig, Ben
Bookings: none

Under-twelves manager's marks out of ten for each player:

Tomasz	6
Connor	7
Matt	6
Ryan	7
Craig	8
Chi	7
Sam	6
Will	8
Jake	9
Yunis	8
Ben	8

Lost

B en felt ridiculous about his plan to escape after the end of the game. Here he was again, doing something mad to avoid talking about his reading problem. It was something *nobody* would ever understand.

As soon as the final whistle went he ran to Ryan and told him: he had to get home and look after the kids. Ryan was about to say something, but Ben was out of there. He didn't have time to stop. People would come over to tell him what a good game he'd had. Then Steve would catch up with him. Ben could see it happening before it did. Steve called it anticipation, said it was good. Ben knew all about anticipation: he was good at it because he couldn't bear the thought of people knowing he couldn't read. He needed to be one step ahead.

This was what he'd learned.

It was only when he was halfway to the dressing rooms that Ben remembered Ryan's mum was giving him a lift back to United's training ground. What would Ryan be thinking of him now? Wouldn't it have been easier just to go with him? Steve might not have said anything to him in front of the lads.

But no. He'd done the right thing.

The priority was avoiding Steve at all costs. He didn't want Steve to know how badly he'd done with his words and he didn't want to have the conversation again.

No way. Not that. If he did he'd be labelled: thicko, dummy, pond life. He knew that because he'd seen it happen to other people. He'd even said it to people himself.

Out of the training complex, Ben got on the first bus he saw that was going downhill. He knew the city was downhill because

Ryan's mum had come uphill to get here, through the city centre.

Ben figured that he could get a train from the centre to United. All he had to do was ask: when was the train, what platform was it on, could he have a ticket? There was nothing to worry about, no need to read.

Except that the further the bus went, the less it looked like Bradford. Bradford had been all back-to-back terraced houses and chimneys and mosques. Out here he could only see bigger houses, parks, then fields. And more fields.

There had been no fields on the way. He was going in completely the wrong direction. He knew it. But what could he do? He was on the bus now; he could hardly get off. So he sat, wearing a face that he hoped looked like he knew where he was going.

*

The bus had been travelling for nearly an hour when Ben saw the white-and-red railway station sign. He got off the bus, saying nothing to the driver. Then he went to the counter in the station and asked for a ticket home.

'That'll take you a while, son,' the woman behind the glass screen said.

'I thought it was close to Bradford.'

'Bradford?' the woman said, leaning

forward. 'This is Skipton, love. You're in the Yorkshire Dales. You only get a train out of here every hour and you just missed one. Then you'll have to change at Leeds.'

Ben couldn't think what to do. So he just stood there. Not crying – just standing.

He got home four hours late. He'd had to get a train to Leeds, then another train and then a bus home, past United's famous stadium.

'WHERE HAVE YOU BEEN?'

His mum was shouting. Loudly.

'I got lost.'

'Lost? I've missed work. Where have you been? I was worried, Ben. I didn't know where on earth you were.'

Ben shrugged and slumped on a seat. His sister came immediately to sit on his knee. Ben stroked her head, so she stroked his head

back. And that was too much for Ben. He burst into tears.

As he cried, he could feel his little sister's arms round his neck and his mum's hand on his back. Then arms and bodies on his legs. His brothers. The whole family.

His mum called this a 'group hug', when the whole family hugged someone. He'd not wanted a group hug for years now. He'd avoided them because they made him feel uncomfortable. But – for once – it felt good. Really good.

And something came to him like a thunderbolt.

He had to do something. Something to stop himself getting into these situations.

Getting lost for four hours.

Hitting team-mates.

Hitting classmates.

Letting his mum down.

Lying to his friends.

He had to do something to support his family and he was going to make a start now.

Practice Makes Perfect

Monday morning.

Ben left home on time again, so his mum would think he was at school. Again.

In fact, he had meant to go back to school that day, but he couldn't. Why bother? He'd only get caught out in the classroom again. There was no hiding his problems. And he didn't fancy seeing Brian Kendrew either. He might as well bunk off.

He took his ball. But the first place he went

was not the park or the pitches: it was the cafe
Steve had taken him to. Ben had the scraps of
paper Steve had given him, ten words on ten
pieces of paper, with the first letter in bold:

Arsenal
Beckham
Coventry
Drogba
Everton
Ferdinand
Goal
Header
Italy
Keegan

What had Steve said?

*Practise. Read them again and again. You know
the word: so learn the first letter. The sound it makes.
Then next time we meet we'll go through it.*

They were bound to meet tonight at training, unless he was going to start playing truant from football as well as school.

Ben sat there with the scraps of paper.

It was hard, really hard.

After a few minutes he had to stop, to get another drink. Tea. He decided it had to be tea. Not because he couldn't say 'Coke' or 'water', but because with Steve it had been tea and tea would help him. It made him think Steve was there with him.

Ben looked around the cafe. It was small, with six benches and steamed-up windows. There was a white counter with a kettle and a rack of chocolate bars. He was the only customer.

Ten minutes later, when he was tired – so tired his head hurt – Ben thought of what else Steve had said.

Learning to read is like getting fit.

Steve said that Ben was not fit when it came to reading. He was about as unfit as you could be. But all he had to do was keep doing a bit of work to get fitter. If he tried every day, going over and over what he needed to, he would get fitter. He would be able to read. Just like he did with football.

So Ben kept trying. He had a coach now. And not just a football coach.

One to One

S teve was sitting in his office, head
down over some paperwork, when
Ben arrived.

Ben watched Steve from the corridor.
United's under-twelves manager was reading
slowly, his finger following the words, his
mouth making out the sounds. It took him
five minutes to read a page. Ben knew that
was a long time. But eventually Steve turned
the page over to read the next.

'Steve?' Ben said, uneasy just watching him.

'Ben.' Steve looked up and smiled a genuine smile. 'Come in. How've you been?'

'OK.'

Steve looked at his watch. 'Not at school?'

Ben shook his head.

Steve nodded. 'Come and sit down. Do you want a drink?'

'Tea, please,' Ben said.

'Tea it is.' Steve smiled.

When the tea was made, steaming on the table, Steve asked Ben about his reading.

'Have you been practising?'

'A bit,' Ben said.

'Do you want to go through it?'

'OK.'

Ben got out the pieces of paper, ready to start. But Steve was on his feet, holding a folder. 'Let's do this outside.' He looked at his watch again. 'On the first team training pitch.'

'What?'

'The first team training pitch.'

'But . . .'

'Only the first team are allowed on there?' Steve said, anticipating Ben's question.

'Yes,' Ben nodded.

'Well, now *you* are,' Steve said.

The pitch was immaculate. The grass was mid-length and so soft underfoot it was like no other pitch Ben had played on.

This grass was only used by the first team – world-famous internationals. They used it for two hours, five days a week. That was it: no other use. It had cost tens of thousands of pounds to lay, and it was watered and treated by the groundsman daily.

Ben felt like he was walking on air.

Steve told Ben to stand on one side of the centre circle, while he stood at the other.

'I've got a copy of the words I gave you on these sheets of paper. I'll hold each one up and play the ball to you. When you play the ball to me you have to tell me what letter it starts with,' Steve said.

'OK.' Ben was excited. The idea of doing letters with Steve had terrified him. But this? Here? It was amazing.

Steve passed the ball to Ben and held up the first paper: Arsenal.

Ben paused. 'It's "a",' he said finally, reading and sounding out the first letter of 'Arsenal' as he knocked the ball straight across the luxury grass. It didn't bobble at all: you could have played golf on this pitch.

'Good. And this one?' Beckham. Steve chipped the ball to him this time. Ben trapped it and slid it back to him.

'"b".'

'What about this?' Coventry. Steve fired it hard but Ben had no trouble. He half volleyed it back.

'"c".'

'Here's another.' Steve's pass was slower. Drogba.

'"dr".' Ben fired it back again.

But Steve trapped the ball. 'Are you sure?'

'"dr",' Ben said again.

'Is that a letter?'

Ben's shoulders dropped. 'No.'

'"d" and "r" make the "dr" sound. So it starts with . . .?'

'"d",' Ben said.

'Great.' Steve chipped the ball to Ben. He held the card up again. 'Drogba?'

'"d",' Ben said.

During the session several of the under-eighteens had stopped to watch. And – instead of feeling ashamed of his reading – Ben felt proud. The under-eighteens were standing at the edge of the pitch but none dared come on it.

Only Ben was allowed to do that.

After the session Ben felt weird. And tired – really tired. Not tired in his body like after a gruelling training run. Tired in his head.

But it had been worth it.

'You did well,' Steve said loudly, as they walked past the under-eighteens. Ben wondered what they must be thinking. That he was getting special training? Something like that.

'Can we talk about school?' Steve said.

Ben shrugged. The sickly feeling came again.

'I want to suggest something,' Steve said.

'What?' Ben asked, trying to keep his voice calm.

'If I talked to your head of year – about your reading – they'd be able to get you some extra help.'

Ben frowned. 'It's OK. Can't we just do this?'

'We can do this. Yes,' Steve said. 'But if you were to get extra help . . .'

'From who?'

Steve paused. It was a long pause. 'Someone to help you, a special teacher,' he said.

Ben felt like he was about to be sick, actually sick. His heart was hammering, his legs like jelly.

'I don't want that,' he said.

'It would help,' Steve nodded. 'It would really help you.'

'No thanks,' Ben said firmly. And seeing Ryan coming up the drive for Monday night training, he added, 'Thanks for today, though. I have to go – my kit's at home.'

'Sure,' Steve said. 'But think about what I've said.'

Ben half smiled, then ran towards Ryan, grinning. And he saw Ryan grin back at him.

It's a Sign

Ryan's mum was driving Ben and Ryan to the next game. Leeds away.

'Where is this place?' she said, getting stressed. They'd been driving around for ages and they were clearly lost.

'I don't know,' Ryan said. 'Leeds United academy – something like that.'

'And where's that?'

'I don't know,' Ryan said again, turning to look at Ben.

'Well, you're a great help,' his mum said.

As they drove, Ryan leaned back over his shoulder and talked to Ben about the Christmas tournament in London next week. They talked about how excited they were and about James – how his form was rubbish and how it was affecting the team.

'What's up with him?' Ben asked.

'I dunno. He's not the player he was earlier in the season,' Ryan said.

'Is it school?'

'Maybe,' Ryan said. 'I'm going to ask him about it when I get him on his own.'

Ryan stopped talking to Ben once his mum shoved a map on to his knee.

'You map read,' she said, 'or I'm driving home. Getting round Leeds is a nightmare.'

While Ryan and his mum were squabbling, Ben took out the pieces of paper Steve had given him.

Arsenal – a.

Beckham – b.

Coventry – c.

Drogba – d.

He went over them again and again. Steve had said he'd have to do this to learn them. Hundreds of times if that's what it took.

The things Ben knew he struggled with were when two letters made the first sound in a word. Like 'd' and 'r' in Drogba. And 't' and 'h' in Theo Walcott. But he was getting there.

'This is awful,' Ryan's mum said. 'I'm taking us home. It's doing my head in. There's no way I can go round all these roads again.'

Ben looked up from the back seat. They were approaching a roundabout. There was a huge road sign, a picture of a roundabout with roads coming off it, each with a name of a place on it.

Ben had never been interested in road signs before, but recently he'd been trying to work out what the words said on them.

'Aaaarrggghhhh,' Ryan's mum shouted in frustration.

Ben looked at the sign. The road to the left was pointing to a place that started with 'Th'. Ben looked again – 'T-h-o-r'. He made the sound in his head. *Thor* . . .

'Does that say Thorpe Arch?' Ben said, pointing at the sign.

'It does, Ben,' Ryan's mum said in a harsh voice. 'So what?'

Ben could see Ryan looking back at him with a big smile on his face.

'That's where they train. Leeds. At Thorpe Arch. It's where we're playing.'

The car swung to the left. Ryan was still grinning at Ben.

'What are you two smirking about now?' Ryan's mum said, giving them a funny look. 'Aaahhh. Here we are. Leeds United. Thorpe Arch. We've found it. Well done, Ben.' Then she added, 'A lot of use you were, Ryan.'

Ben couldn't speak. He felt as if a fireworks display was going off inside him. Extreme happiness. He'd not felt this happy before.

Leeds Away

T he game against Leeds went well for
the first half.

United seemed to have a new
dimension to their game. All the practising
they'd done around knowing where their
team-mates were and anticipating what
would happen next was paying off.

They were knocking it about and keeping
the ball for several passes.

But Leeds were good too. Very good.
Their youth team was famous for being one
of the best.

Before the game, Ben had tried to get to talk to Steve alone, but he'd not got the chance. Steve was busy trying to deal with Ryan's mum, who was moaning about getting lost – and asking why the club didn't provide parents with proper directions.

So Ben decided to leave it until after the game.

And he knew that this was one match he wasn't going to leave quickly at the end. He was still excited about having read the word on the sign. He'd get Steve on his own, then tell him the news.

And tell him something else too.

The first half was goalless, United and Leeds cancelling each other out. But in the second half the game opened up. It was classic end-to-end stuff, with Jake and Yunis causing Leeds real problems. But Leeds were quick, that was the thing. Once Steve had seen how quick they really were, he told the team to play deeper, so they wouldn't be as exposed to the counter-attack.

'Play on the break,' he'd said at half-time. 'We've practised this. Keep the ball in defence. Pack the midfield. Then when we

get possession, get the ball out to Jake or Ben, and then up to Yunis and Will.'

After one such counter-attack, halfway through the second period, the game changed.

Ben and James had held back as most of the team had rushed forward in search of a goal. But the attack had broken down, the ball cleared by Leeds. To Ben.

Ben trapped the ball in the centre circle. He tried to focus on where his team-mates were, remembering what Steve had taught them. But Leeds players were closing him down from their half.

Ben knew he had only one option, really: to play it back to James. But James was not playing well. He was making a lot of unforced errors and he'd missed the last game. Now several Leeds players were streaming towards them. And Ben hesitated.

What could he do? Play it back to James and risk him making a mistake? Or try to chip it over the Leeds players to one of his team-mates stranded up field?

Ben chose to chip it.

He'd lost confidence in James.

But the ball was knocked down by a Leeds player immediately and Ben found himself out of the game. It was four against one now. James was totally exposed, thanks to Ben.

United players tried to catch the Leeds attackers, but it was too late.

The Leeds striker drew Tomasz off his line, then side-footed the ball to his right.

James tried to reach it, but another player in white was on to it.

One–nil.

And that's how it stayed, leaving Ben furious with himself.

He'd lost United the game.

Sunday 18 December
Leeds 1 United 0
Goals: none
Bookings: Craig, James, Will

Under-twelves manager's marks out of ten for each player:

Tomasz	6
Connor	6
James	5
Ryan	6
Craig	6
Chi	6
Sam	6
Will	5
Jake	6
Yunis	5
Ben	4

Reading the Game

After Ben had apologized to James – and the rest of the team – for his mistake, he waited in the dressing room for Steve. The players drifted away to another Sunday afternoon.

When Steve came, he offered Ben a lift home, which was what Ben had been hoping for. He told Ryan's mum.

'Oh, right. Got a better offer, have you? My old banger's not good enough for you now. Well, don't be sure I'll offer you a lift again.'

Ben smiled, but Ryan frowned.

Ben felt glad she wasn't his mum.

'Sorry about that pass,' Ben said.

They were cruising through the streets in
Steve's car. It was a Mercedes. You couldn't
hear the engine or feel any of the bumps on
the road. It was a nice car, a very nice car.

Ben said nothing about the road sign. Every time he wanted to, he felt overwhelmed by emotion and fear, almost like he wasn't sure he could actually say it.

'That's OK, Ben,' Steve said, in response to his apology. 'You know it was a mistake. We all make them. I'm sure you'll learn from it.'

Ben nodded. 'I will,' he said.

'How's everything else?' Steve asked.

Ben paused. He could feel tears forming in his eyes. He decided to say it – now. He had to.

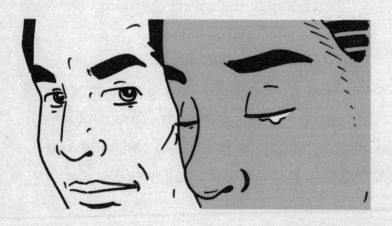

'I read a sign,' he said.

'What?' Steve looked at him and quickly slowed down to stop the car. Once they were stationary, Steve just looked at Ben, not speaking.

'We were coming up through Leeds,' Ben said, 'and Ryan's mum was lost.'

'I gathered that.' Steve grinned.

Ben smiled. 'And I saw a sign – "Thorpe". I read the word "Thorpe". And I knew that Leeds train at Thorpe Arch, so I could tell her where it was.'

Steve clapped his hands. 'That's brilliant, Ben. How did you feel?'

'I still feel it.'

'So how *do* you feel?'

'Amazing,' Ben said, wiping his eyes.

Steve nodded. 'I'm proud of you, son. Well done. That is absolutely amazing. And it's down to you – and all that hard work.'

Steve's hands went to his key to switch the engine on.

'There's something else,' Ben said.

'Right,' Steve nodded.

'I want to get help at school. I want them to help me.'

Steve smiled. Then Ben saw his eyes go a

bit glassy and he felt Steve's hand on his shoulder.

'Thanks,' Ben said.

Steve just nodded. Then he started the ignition of the car.

And they were off.

Thank Yous

Thank you, as always, to my wife, Rebecca, and daughter, Iris, for their ongoing support and encouragement with my books. But to Rebecca, in particular, for having the idea for this book. And for reading it at its various stages. And also special thanks to Iris for being the brains behind chapter two.

Thanks to Ralph Newbrook for great training drills for the team. And to Sophie Hannah and James Nash for excellent feedback on the novel in its first draft.

Thanks, as always, to Burnley FC for allowing me to spend time at their training ground and to get some of the facts about academy football straight.

And to Nikki Woodman, neighbour and friend, who helped me make the story of Ben and his reading difficulties as realistic as I could.

Saying that, all football and literacy errors in the book are mine.

Finally, I'd like to thank everyone at Puffin for the wonderful work they do: including Sarah Hughes, Alison Dougal, Helen Levene, Wendy Tse, Reetu Kabra, Adele Minchin, Louise Heskett, Sarah Kettle, Tom Sanderson and everyone in the rights team. And thanks to Brian Williamson for the great cover image and illustrations.

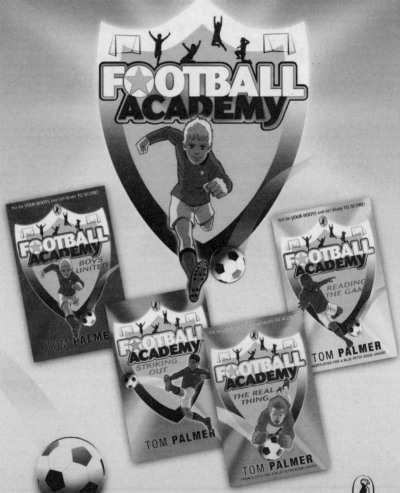

It all started with a Scarecrow

Puffin is well over sixty years old.
Sounds ancient, doesn't it? But Puffin has never been
so lively. We're always on the lookout for the next big
idea, which is how it began all those years ago.

Penguin Books was a big idea from the mind of
a man called Allen Lane, who in 1935 invented
the quality paperback and changed the world.
**And from great Penguins, great Puffins grew,
changing the face of children's books forever.**

The first four Puffin Picture Books were hatched in 1940 and the
first Puffin story book featured a man with broomstick arms called
Worzel Gummidge. In 1967 Kaye Webb, Puffin Editor, started the
Puffin Club, promising to **'make children into readers'.**
She kept that promise and over 200,000 children became
devoted Puffineers through their quarterly installments of
Puffin Post, which is now back for a new generation.

Many years from now, we hope you'll look back and
remember Puffin with a smile. **No matter what your age
or what you're into, there's a Puffin for everyone.**
The possibilities are endless, but one thing is for sure:
whether it's a picture book or a paperback, a sticker book
or a hardback, **if it's got that little Puffin
on it – it's bound to be good.**